Iktomi
and the
Boulder

Orchard Books
New York

Iktomi
and the
Boulder

a Plains Indian story

retold and illustrated
by PAUL GOBLE

for Robert

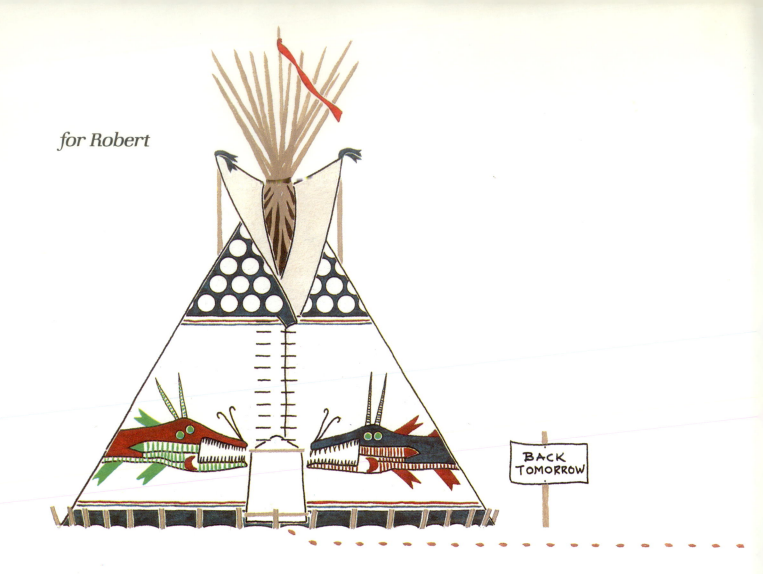

References

Ella Deloria, *Dakota Texts*, Publications of the American Ethnological Society, Vol. 14, New York, 1932; George Bird Grinnell, *Blackfoot Lodge Tales*, Charles Scribner's Sons, New York, 1892; *By Cheyenne Campfires*, Yale University Press, New Haven, 1926; J. Frank Dobie, *The Voice of the Coyote*, Hammond and Hammond, London, 1950; Henry Tall Bull and Tom Weist, *Veho*, Montana Reading Publications, Billings, 1971; R. D. Theisz, editor, *Buckskin Tokens*, North Plains Press, Aberdeen, 1975; Stith Thompson, *Tales of the American Indians*, Indiana University Press, Bloomington, 1929; John Stands in Timber and Margot Liberty, *Cheyenne Memories*, Yale University Press, New Haven, 1967.

Text and illustrations © 1988 by Paul Goble. All rights reserved. No part of this book may be reproduced or transmitted in any form or by any means, electronic or mechanical, including photocopying, recording or by any information storage or retrieval system, without permission in writing from the Publisher. Orchard Books, A division of Franklin Watts, Inc., 387 Park Avenue South, New York, New York 10016. Manufactured in the United States of America. The text of this book is set in 22 pt. Zapf Book Light. The illustrations are India ink and watercolor, reproduced in combined line and halftone. Library of Congress Cataloging-in-Publication Data. Goble, Paul. Iktomi and the boulder. Summary: Iktomi, a Plains Indian trickster, attempts to defeat a boulder with the assistance of some bats, in this story which explains why the Great Plains are covered with small stones. 1. Dakota Indians—Legends. 2. Indians of North America—Great Plains—Legends. [1. Dakota Indians—Legends. 2. Indians of North America—Great Plains—Legends] I. Title. E99.D1G63 1988 398.2'08997 [E] 87-35789 ISBN 0-531-05760-7 ISBN 0-531-08360-8 (lib. bdg.) ISBN 0-531-07023-9 (pbk.) 10 9 8 7 6 5 4 3 2 1

About Iktomi

Iktomi is the hero of many amusing stories. Iktomi (pronounced *eek-toe-me*) is his Sioux name; he stars in similar stories from all over North America and is known by various names: Coyote, Sinti, Old Man Napi, Nanabozo, Sinkalip, Wihio, Veho, and others. Iktomi, or Ikto, is very clever, with unusual magical powers, but he is also very stupid, a liar, and a mischief-maker. He is forever trying to get the better of others but is himself usually fooled. The mention of Iktomi's name makes people smile, for he is always up to no good and always getting himself into trouble. He is beyond the realm of moral values. He lacks all sincerity. Tales about Iktomi remind us that unsociable and chaotic behavior is never far below the surface. We can see ourselves in him.

Iktomi is also credited with greater things: in many of the older stories the Creator entrusts him with much of Creation. People say that what seem to be the "mistakes" and "irrational" aspects of Creation, such as earthquakes, floods, disease, flies, and mosquitos, were surely made by Iktomi.

There is no single "correct" version of these stories; story-tellers kept to certain familiar themes and wove variations around them. Tales with a moral, but without any sermon, they were told in informal language, because Iktomi has no respect for the precise use of words. All the stories start in the same way: "Iktomi was walking along..." The words suggest right from the start that Iktomi is idle and aimless, with nothing better to do than to cause mischief for our amusement.

A Note for the Reader

Iktomi's thoughts, printed in small type, need not be read aloud but can perhaps be read when looking at the pictures with children. Readers may even have their own ideas to add about what Iktomi is thinking.

Where the text changes to italic, readers may want to let their listeners make remarks about what Iktomi is doing. This is quite in keeping with traditional Iktomi story-telling; listeners are expected to make their own comments and rude remarks about Iktomi. And then the story-teller lifts a forefinger for silence, and goes on with the story....

Iktomi was walking along....
*Every story about Iktomi
starts this way.*

Iktomi was walking along.
It was a beautiful morning.
Iktomi was going to visit
his friends and relations
in the next village.

My feather bonnet

I'm looking my
very best today.

My fan

My tobacco bag

My blanket

I bet the birds wish
they had all my feathers.

I'll look great at the
dance tonight.

He was feeling happy with himself.
He had painted his face
and was wearing all his very best clothes.
Doesn't he look like a dandy?

I really am very
good-looking. I look
like a real chief.

"How handsome I look," he was thinking.
"Everyone will be impressed.
All the girls
will want me to notice them."
Iktomi is forever showing off—and then
always getting into trouble.
He never learns.
The birds and animals
stopped to look as he passed.
Iktomi was feeling much too important
to notice them.
He never noticed
that they were laughing at him!

I'll pick it up again
on my way back.

"Grandfather," he said to the boulder,
"Grandfather Boulder, I feel sorry for you.
You are terribly sunburnt
from sitting here so long in the sun.
You have given me shade.
I'm generous, too.
I give you my blanket
to keep the sun off you. Take it."
He wasn't really generous at all, was he?

Iktomi spread his blanket over the boulder,
and went on his way.

After a while he noticed
dark thunder clouds gathering
like mountains behind him.
"I might need my blanket after all,"
he thought. "Rain would spoil
my beautiful clothes."

"I did give it," he said to himself
as he walked back.
"A gift is a gift. Still,
I need it. Anyway, it's much too nice
a blanket just to leave on a rock."

"Boulder," he said,
"you don't need my blanket.
You are only a rock.
The sun can't burn you any more.
I was only lending it to you."
That's not true, is it?

Iktomi snatched the blanket off the boulder.

Thank goodness I thought
to bring my blanket!

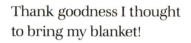

He had not gone far
when it started to thunder and rain.
He sat down and sheltered
under his blanket.

Soon, above the rumble of thunder,
he heard a different sound:
it seemed to shake the earth—
a regular *thump-crash-bump-*
thump-bump-crash—
"That doesn't sound like thunder,"
he thought.

Whatever's that?

He peeped out from under his blanket;
that great boulder was bouncing
and crashing across the prairie
straight toward him!

Iktomi dropped his blanket
and ran in absolute terror.

"I must get to the top of the hill,"
he muttered.
"The boulder cannot go uphill."
He was wrong!
The boulder pounded end over end
right to the top.

"I must get across the river,"
he panted.
"That boulder will get stuck in the mud."
Iktomi ran down toward the river,
the boulder bounding and thumping
close at his heels.

Anyone can outwit a rock!

That rock has
a terrible temper.

He ran this way.
He ran that way.

He just could not escape
from the boulder.

He splashed across the river,
gasping for breath,
and scrambled out on the far bank
and fell down exhausted.
The boulder jumped the river
in one mighty bound.
Before Iktomi could get up again,
the boulder rolled on top of his legs,
and stopped.

Now what is Iktomi going to do?
Is it the end of the story?

Help!
Get off me! Do you hear?
What are you doing?

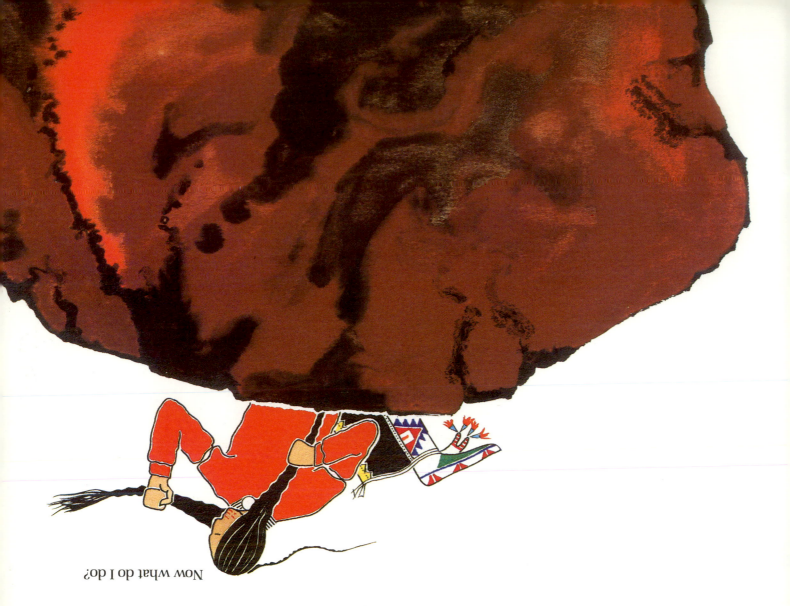

Now what do I do?

Iktomi could not move.
He struggled. He screamed.
He hit the boulder. He pleaded.
He cried. It made no difference;
the boulder did not move.

Some buffaloes heard Iktomi
and came to have a look.
"My younger brothers," Iktomi said.
Iktomi has no respect.
He calls everyone "younger brother."
"Younger brothers," he said
to the buffaloes, "please help me.
I was just climbing around on this boulder
when it rolled over onto my legs.
See, I cannot move. Roll it off me."

That wasn't true, was it?

The bulls got their horns underneath
and h-e-a-v-e-d and s-h-o-v-e-d,
but they could not move the boulder
even a little bit.
The elk, the antelope and the bears
saw what was happening.
They came to help.

Come on—*push!*
Don't be so feeble.

Even the prairie dogs and the smallest
of the four-legged ones joined in.
They could not roll the boulder
off Iktomi's legs.

They gave up
and wandered off.

What's the matter with you?
For goodness sake, *push!*

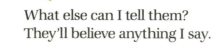

What else can I tell them?
They'll believe anything I say.

Darkness came, and the bats appeared
with the rising moon.
"Ho! My younger brothers!"
Iktomi called out to the bats.
"This boulder has been saying rude things
about you.
He said you are so ugly
that you don't dare show yourselves
during the daytime.
He said that you sleep upside-down
because you don't know your 'up side'
from your 'down side.'
He said some other things,
but I simply cannot repeat them."

*Of course Iktomi was making up stories
again, wasn't he?*

It made the bats cross.
More and more of them gathered.
"I told this boulder that he ought
to know better than to insult
his good-looking relatives.
He even said that you don't know whether
you are birds or animals,
two-legged or four-legged.
'Furry Birds,' he called you.
What a dreadful thing to say—"

The bats were furious.
Suddenly they started hitting the boulder.
They darted this way and that,
and each time they struck,
pieces of the boulder broke off.
"Yes! *Furry Birds* he called you,"
Iktomi shouted.

Bats and pieces of rock
flew in every direction.

Ha! That's done it!
I always knew I could get even
with that stupid rock!

"Don't know your 'up side'
from your 'down side'!"
Iktomi yelled.
The bats swooped at the boulder
and knocked off pieces
until there was nothing left but little chips.

"That's right," Iktomi said to the bats.
"You taught that boulder a lesson."

Iktomi went on his way again....

*What do you think
Iktomi will get up to next?*

Let me think:
what shall I do now?

*This story also explains why
bats have flattened faces,
and why there are rocks
scattered all over the Great Plains.*